Mo Willems

Presents

That Is NOT a Good Idea!

WALKER BOOKS

AND SUBSIDIARIES

LONDON · BOSTON · SYDNEY · AUCKLAND

"What luck!"

"Dinner!"

"Excuse me.

Would you care

to go

for a stroll?"

"Hmm ...

sure!"

"That is NOT a good idea!"

"Would you care

to continue our walk

into the deep,

dark woods?"

"Sounds fun!"

"That is REALLY NOT a good idea!"

"Would you care

to visit my nearby

kitchen?"

"I would love to!"

"That is REALLY, REALLY, REALLY NOT a good idea!"

"Would you care

to boil some water

for soup?"

"Certainly.

I do love soup!"

"That is **REALLY, REALLY, REALLY NOT** a good idea!"

"Would you care

to look at my soup?

A key ingredient

is missing."

"That is
REALLY,
REALLY,
REALLY,
REALLY
NOT
a good idea!"

"Oh –

a key ingredient

IS missing."

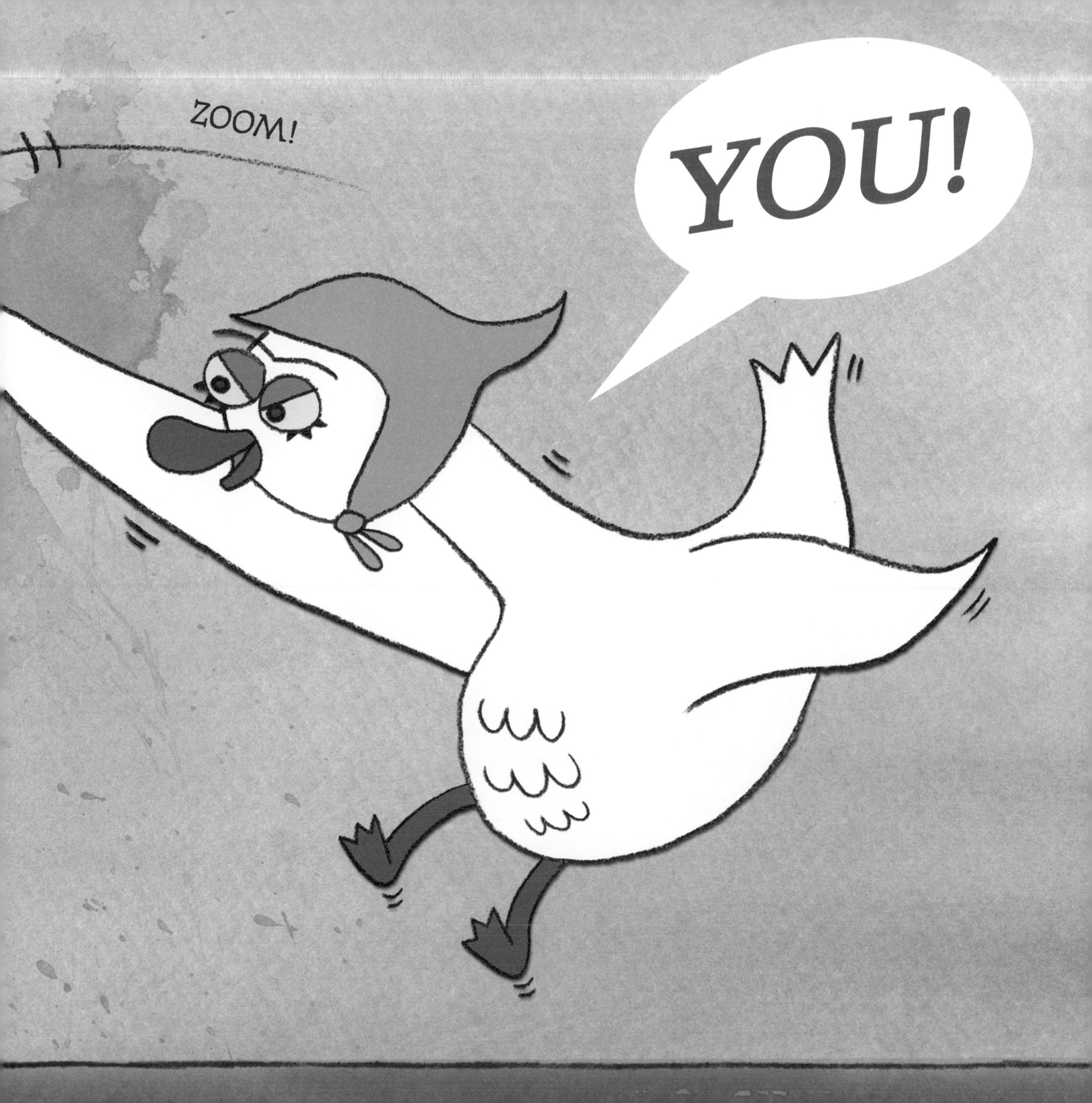
ZOOM!
YOU!

The END.